"Frost, You Say?"

"Frost, You Say?"

A YANKEE MONOLOGUE

TEXT BY
Marshall J. Dodge 3rd

WITH
Walter Howe

PHOTOGRAPHS BY
Mary Eastman

DOWN EAST BOOKS / CAMDEN, MAINE

Library of Congress Catalog Card No.: 80-69082

ISBN 0-89272-105-7

Printed in the United States of America
by Capital City Press

This book
is
dedicated to
nineteenth-century
Maine
which is laughing at us.

PREFACE

"Frost, You Say?" is a story which used to be told by Dr. Horace Stevens of Cambridge, Massachusetts. He performed it before audiences at the St. Botolph Club and made several recordings of it, though the origin of the story is not clear. Perhaps Dr. Stevens composed it himself. In all likelihood, however, it has been passed down through a long line of storytellers in the men's clubs of Boston. From "Waddy" Longfellow to Alan Bemis, they specialized in Maine stories, though many themes were borrowed from other traditions. *"Frost, You Say?"* is no doubt one of these, for it has the polish of a turn-of-the-century parlor recitation or a vaudeville monologue rather than the rough-and-ready quality of a folk story.

When it was decided to produce the story in book form, inspiration came from the works of Keith Jennison; *The Maine Idea,* for instance. A piece such as *"Frost, You Say?"* does not produce much effect in print unless each line is animated as it would be in the telling of it. The high photograph-to-text ratio provides the animation here, as it does in the Jennison books.

Walter Howe was an obvious choice to portray the main character, just as he had been for the filmed version called *A Down East Smile-In,* a three-part Public Television series which appeared in 1970. Since the story is infinitely expandable, for the book it was decided to add many of Mr. Howe's own descriptions of his daily activities.

Parts of the story, however, bear no resemblance to Mr. Howe's real life. For example, he does not sleep upstairs, but rather on the ground floor, in a room which does not appear in the photographs.

Furthermore, the real Mr. Howe would have answered the question about frost with a "Yes" or a "No." Parts of the old story, as Dr. Stevens told it, do not appear in the book at all. Because Mr. Howe has no dining room, for example, that part of the Stevens version describing it is deleted.

Walter Howe was born on August 18, 1894, in Camden, Maine, in a house which was replaced by his present dwelling in 1907. His paternal great-grandfather, Jonah Howe, lived on the present property as did his grandfather Abner and his father Herbert. His mother was born in North Haven, Maine, and her father ran a packet boat off that island until 1864.

Walter's family earned its living from farm produce; eggs, butter, beef, pork, chicken, apples, wood and maple syrup, all of which they sold door-to-door or shipped to Boston. When Walter's older brother Oscar died in 1952, Walter began to specialize in blueberry harvesting and made the farm more profitable than it has ever been, even in his father's time.

The Howe farm no longer has 400 chickens and 27 head of cattle, including two pair of working oxen and milking cows. There are no longer any pigs, or horses. The cow and calf that appear in these photographs have been sold because they had become too much for Mr. Howe to care for. Despite these curtailments, Walter Howe's farm is still very much alive.

—MARSHALL J. DODGE, 3RD

8

"Frost, you say?
You asked me if I had any frost to my place this morning?

Well now, let me tell you.
This morning I woke up about five o'clock.
Never been a lay-a-bed in the Howe family.

I jumped into my boots, pulled on my pants, and stepped over
to that wash basin of mine. I generally wash my face and hands,
dry them off, and head down over them stairs.

Now them stairs.
I don't want none of those steep narrow stairs where you
break your darned neck going up and down them like a ladder.
My stairs have got twelve-inch treads and only five-inch risers.
And you don't wear no holes in the middle of them either,
'cause they are made out of solid oak.

And alongside them stairs I got a red cherry bannister
and at the foot, a newell post made out of curly ash.
I tell you, the combination of red cherry and curly ash
looks just fine in the early morning light
when you come down to do your chores.

At the foot of them stairs, I got a settin' room.
And in the center of that settin' room I got a Jewel stove.
At night, before I go to bed, I lay on a couple of sticks
of maple. In the morning I throw a log in on a nice
bed of coals and I get her roaring in no time.

Over in the corner of that settin' room of mine
I got me a red plush sofy.
It may be a bit wore out now, but the comfort
is the same as it always was. You know, sometimes
I don't think nothing of lying on that sofy reading 'til
almost 8:30 before I go to bed.

Beyond the settin' room is my kitchen.
In the center of that kitchen is a big black Home Clarion stove.
It has five or six controls onto it and it takes more than
a teaspoonful of brains to operate it,
but maybe that's why there aren't
so many of them stoves around today.

I can cook five dishes on that Clarion, all at once,
and have them come out perfect.
The front of the stove is for searing, that's where I try out bacon.
The back part is for simmering, its where I make soup from bones.
On the left is the waiting place
where the pork waits for the beans
and the butter waits for the clams.
And on the right is where I thaw out my shellac in the spring.

For breakfast, I warmed some kidney beans I had baked last week.
These Kentucky Wonder pole beans are the mildest tasting
beans I raise. I parboil them and then bake them overnight
with mustard, pork and a little maple sugar.
Then every morning I heat them up again.
I always say a man who is not regular in his habits
won't amount to nothing.

I had some rolls for breakfast, too.
I soured a bowl of milk on the stove, mixed it
with baking soda and flour, and cut up the dough to fit my roll tin.
I try to keep the oven at a steady 300° or over,
but I don't time them.
I don't even look at them while they're baking.

I just pull them out when they're done.

I always wash the dishes right after eating,
before I lose my courage.
I pour some hot water from the kettle into a pan and
finish them fast. Can't let them stand around dirty.
Got to have something to eat off of next meal.

After I finished my breakfast, I went outside
to look at the rain gauge.
Been doing that for the past twenty years,
and I'll be darned if I know why.

This year it rained over thirty-two inches from April to October.
Last year, it rained sixteen inches in that time.

Lucky I'm a carpenter.
Next year I'll build an ark.

I always look at my thermometer, too.
The mercury dropped so low for a spell last winter,
I thought it was going to drag the whole house
over onto its side.

I brought the cat over to the barn to get fed.

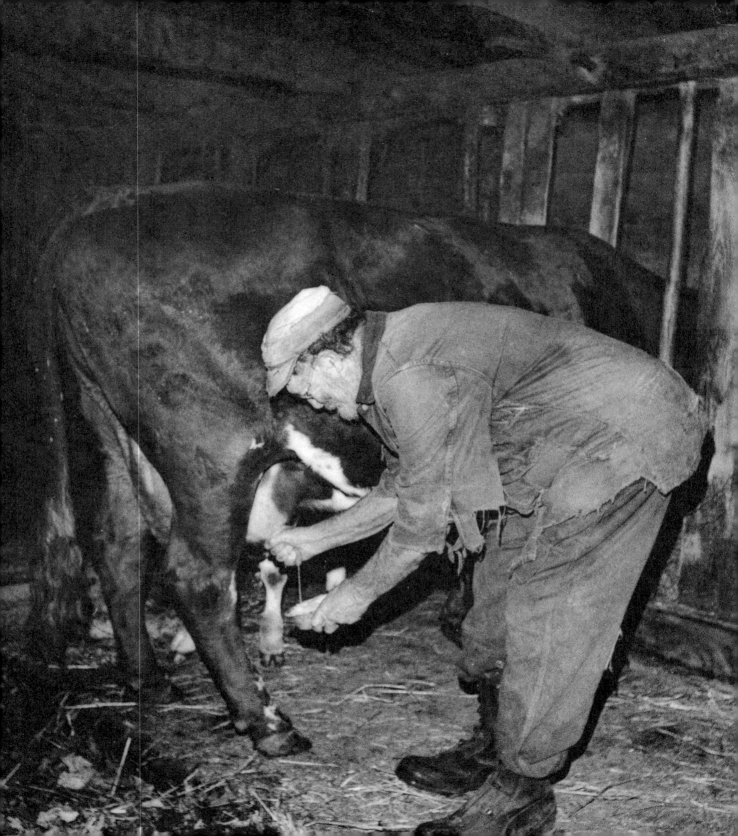

That cat has her own cow
and her own saucer . . .

. . . and her own farmer, I guess.

I went out to the garden to pick the last of them
Kentucky Wonder pole beans of mine.
They're the same beans that father bought in 1917.
You'd think they'd run down over the years and get weaker.
But as far as I can tell, they're stronger than ever.

Either that or it's me who's running down.

The rats ate my seed corn last year.
This year, they'll have to be acrobats to get at it.

50

The last of the pears needed picking.

I hadn't sprayed them, so they were all shrunk up and puckery.
'Course they aren't going to kill you,

but they may spoil your disposition.

Only last month I went down to the lower field to repair the wall.

Next month I will put on the banking.
I put down hay and then spruce bows.
It keeps the cold out of the foundation . . . they say.

Well, my grandfather did it, and so did my father
. . . and I guess I'd better, too.

Most people rake leaves just to clear their dooryards.

I rake my lawn so my calf can sleep comfortable.
She likes leaves better than straw.

Seems kind of noisy to me.

In the old days, when we had twenty-seven head of cattle,
they'd keep the grass down in places even I couldn't cut.
Now I have to take out my scythe to cut some places
that the mowing machine misses.
Wish I had a few chickens 'cause for keeping the grass down,
they're better than lawnmowers.

My grandnephew says I look like the grim reaper when I mow.

I guess that will give us something to talk about
when we finally meet.

That reminds me of my brother Oscar.
He used to buy his overalls three sizes too large
so he could cut the bottoms off the pants
to make a hat.

Now come the fall, I got to sharpen my axe
so I can look for a tree in the woodlot.

Soon as I find it,

I just chop that tree

down . . .

. . . to make a new axe handle.

Three weeks ago Elizabeth Harkness asked me
if she could go blueberrying in my fields on the hill
near the woodlot. I told her she could take all she wanted.

She came back at the end of the day with a dozen berries.
'Well, Elizabeth,' I said, 'just like I told you,
all those berries on the hill are yours.'

I like to go dowsing up on the hill to the north,
not looking for water, but just for practice.
All I ever do with those sticks is practice.
Got all the water I need.

Course I did find an axe head
I had lost forty-two years ago
in the cow pasture.
Guess them sticks have got some use after all.

Then again, come to think about it,
that axe head was all rusted out.

This morning,
when I put the cow out in that same pasture, and shut the gate . . .

. . . I just happened to look down at the ground
and, do you know, there on the grass was . . .

. . . just a little mite of frost."